HOSS
WOMAN

by

Carolyn Gilman Middleton Guyer

Chapter One

Thirteen year old Hester Harmon dragged her bare feet through the hot sand as she pulled her three year old sister Mary down the road to town. Zeke and Billy, her brothers, chased each other around but Hester knew they would calm down soon. It was three miles to town. She had dressed the children as best she could but nothing fit. Hester had used the last of the water to straighten their hair. Pa had taken the comb and everything not nailed down when he ran off with a dance hall dolly. Hester cared for her siblings as best she could, but she needed food and money. She was going to town to look for work.

"I'm hungry, " said Billy.

"Me too," whined Zeke.

Hester knew that if her Ma could see them now she would be devastate. She remembered Ma and Pa laughing and dancing. They were a handsome couple and in love, but then her mother died birthing Mary. Hester had tried to help her but by the time her Pa got home, Lucinda was gone. Then Pa started drinking; stopped tending to the livestock and garden; he sold things – her mother's things. He didn't buy food and often wasn't home for several days.

Hester went to town and found her Pa blurry-eyed and drunk. Sheriff Lawson had brought her home on his chestnut horse with saddle bags full of potatoes, flour, sugar and coffee. She picked wild berries in the meadow and Billy fastened a rabbit trap and went fishing. Then the brook dried up. Hester sat by the wet patch and bawled like a baby. She straightened her shoulders, rubbed her snotty nose on her sleeve and made plans. Her Ma had told her if she ever needed help, to look at the end of her own arm.

Hester laid sleepy Mary under a tall saguaro at the edge of town and told the boys to sit there until she came back. First, she went to the General Store but Mr. Feathers said he didn't need help. Hester went to the cafe, but Mrs. Higgins looked down her nose at her and told her to go away. Hester went to Sheriff Lawson's Office and was surprised to see the children there, laughing and eating big bowls of stew.

"I was going to ride to your cabin this mornings," the Sheriff said with a grin, "but I found these bad outlaws and I had to arrest them and sentence them to eat stew. I'm so glad the leader of this gang showed up and turned herself in."

Mrs. Lawson came in. She was the banker's daughter and was a stern-faced lady dressed in beautiful clothes. Hester thought she was bossy and not friendly at all.

"My, my," she said, "Looks like someone needs bathing and new clothes." She herded the children out, not even glancing t Hester.

"I need a job," Hester said to the Sheriff. "I went to the store and cafe. Do you need a deputy?"

"Well, the only places left are the stable and the saloon. Maybe you could clean them, but that's nasty work."

Petey, the Sheriff's deputy, burst through the door.

"Fight at the saloon," he said and ran out.

The Sheriff buckled on his gun and left.

Hester went to the stables. No one was there except

one old nag staring dejectedly at her. Hester fed him hay and filled the water pail. She wandered towards the saloon.

The Sheriff and Petey were dragging the swamper, One-Eyed Joe, out by his boots and down the wooden sidewalk towards the cemetery. The bartender, Faro, stood in the doorway wiping his hands on a dirty apron. He had always been kind to Hester.

"I need a job, Mr. Faro," she said politely.

Faro looked at her too-small dress and bare feet and messy hair. He continued to wipe his hands and turn away, but then turned back.

"Looks like I need a swamper," he said. "After the drunks go home, the floors have to be washed, spittoons cleaned and the swamper cooks some stew if anyone is hungry."

"I can do that," Hester said eagerly.

"Go upstairs; knock on the second door and tell Marie I sent you to clean up. Pay is two bits a week, all you can eat and you can sleep in the storeroom.

Hester ran up the stairs quickly; before Faro changed his mind.

When Marie sleepily answered the door, she said, "I'm Hester and I am the new swamper. Faro sent me up so you can make me presentable."

Marie looked at the tall, thin girl wearing a rag; no shoes and her hair was a dirty mess.

"What happened to One-Eyed?" she asked.

"Dead," Hester said.

"Go behind the screen, take off those clothes and wash up," Marie ordered.

She found a tub with cold water, some soap, which she hadn't seen in a long while. It smelled nice. She looked in the mirror and was shocked at how skinny and messy she looked.

Marie threw some clothes over the screen and told her to put them on.

The underclothes were big and the dress was blue calico. She tied the sash tightly so it didn't look so big on her.

Hester came around the screen and Marie adjusted the clothes and then started to brush Hester's tangled hair. Marie pulled up the sides and rolled them to the back, pinning them carefully. She left the back hair hanging to her waist. Marie found an old pair of black slippers; they almost fit.

"I hope you make better stew than One-Eyed,"

Marie grumbled.

"You betcha," said Hester grinning. "Thanks for your help."

There were four cowboys, dusty and wanting whiskey. They stared.

"Boys," said Faro. "This is my new swamper Hester."

One cowboy removed his hat. "I'm gonna be spilling a lot of drinks<" he grinned.

After the drinks were served, Faro took her to the kitchen and showed her around. He gave her some coins and told her to buy what she needed.

Hester found meat and flour and sugar and some dried vegetables. The pots were filthy, so she scrubbed them with sand outside the back door. She lugged water from the well and stoked the fire. She whipped up some biscuits but there was no oven, so she cooked them in a fry pan by placing it over the steaming pot of stew.

Faro called for two orders of stew and she added two biscuits. Hester fretted about the children.

Faro came to the kitchen and looked into the stew pot.

"Better get more supplies," he said.

Hester hung her apron on the peg by the back door. The Sheriff's Office was closed so she ran to his house.

"Are the children here?" asked Hester when Betty Sue answered her knock.

Her brothers and sister came running, chattering and laughing. They were clean and had on new clothes. Mary was hugging a rag doll.

"Can they stay here tonight?" she asked the Sheriff's wife anxiously.

"Yes," said Betty Sue.

Hester kissed and hugged the children. She hurried to Feathers store and bought her supplies.

Faro was standing outside the back door in the alley.

"Thought you'd run off," he grumbled.

Hester was busy all evening, running back and forth, making more biscuits and stew. She was exhausted; but she had to clean the floor and spittoons; then wash the dishes. Her arms ached and her feet hurt. She went to the storage room and was dismayed to see there was no lock. She fell on the smelly pallet on the floor and was asleep instantly.

When she woke in the morning, she went to the door. It was locked from the outside. The door was the only outlet except for a small oilskin window high up near the pitch of the roof. There were barrels of whiskey and beer; her pallet and a washstand on a rickety stand. She laid back down and cried herself to sleep.

A thump at the door woke her and two burly men opened it and rolled in several barrels.

"Sorry, miss," the first man said. "Didn't know you slept here and the door was bolted."

When the men were leaving, Hester called, "Wait. I don't have much room. Could you stack those barrels on top of each other?"

The men did as she asked.

Hester worked hard all day, preparing food, carrying water, cleaning spills in the bar and dodging cowboys.

She was taking a breather when she heard a knock on the alley door. It was her brother Billy. He threw his arms around her and hugged her tightly.

"I came to say goodbye," he said sadly. Hester was

shocked. "The Sheriff arranged for me to go to work on a farm owned by John Hutchins – just outside of town. He'll give me room and board and he'll let me visit Zeke, Mary and you when he comes to town."

Hester hugged him close and whispered how much she would miss him, but it was a good thing and they would all be together someday.

Faro called for bowls of soup and Billy quickly slipped out the back, giving a sorry little wave.

Hester worked until the saloon was empty and then mopped the floor. She took a chair with her to the storeroom and she put it under the door handle. Several cowboys had made innuendos and suggestions. She was scared so she took a knife and hid it under her pallet. That made her feel better.

She was washing her apron when Faro opened the

door. He smelled like whiskey and he put his arms around her, dragging her into the storeroom.

"No," she cried. She tried to get to the door, but Faro slammed it before she got there. He threw her onto the pallet and before he could lie on her, she drew out the knife she had hidden and stabbed him. He yelled in pain and then was still.

Hester moved to the whiskey barrels and hauled herself up. She could reach the window standing tiptoe on the top barrel. She ripped the oilcloth off the window and boosted herself up. Fear gripped her as she looked down; it was a long way. She hung out the window by her fingertips; took a deep breath and let go. Pain shot through both her feet and up her legs; she lay on her back stunned and wracked with pain. A large shadow bent over her and Hester was picked up by her armpits and held against a soft body. A horrid stench filled her nostrils and a cape made from something hairy covered her. The person lumbered slowly away with Hester hanging from it. Hester was about to yell when she heard Sheriff Lawson's voice.

"Coffee Kate," he called, "Coffee Kate. Did you see a young girl jump out that window?"

"What did she do?' the nasty, stinking hulk asked.

"She knifed Faro," the Sheriff said. "I guess she went crazy and he wants her in jail."

"Don't see no one," said Kate in a gravelly voice. "Leaving now."

Hester's feet and legs burned and ached. She dozed off with the gentle swinging motion and when she woke, she was laying on the ground. Both her feet were bound with cloth and sticks and a fire burned. The large woman was snoozing across the fire, snoring lightly.

Coffee Kate opened one eye and said, "They call me Coffee Kate cuz I make the best coffee in the world. I'm leaving for the mountains to trap beaver and muskrat. Wanna come along? I'll give you half the take; be coming back in springtime."

Hester nodded and dozed until Coffee Kate lifted her to the back of a cart being driven by two long haired cattle. Her feet felt better and she was hungry.

Seeing she was awake, Kate opened a paper packet on the seat beside her and handed the contents back to her. She gobbled it quickly. Kate motioned for Hester to move to the front and Hester crawled over the foodstuffs and onto the wooden bench. Kate handed her a tankard of coffee and Hester guzzled it down. It was delicious and she smacked her lips which made Kate laugh; a deep, ponderous sound.

Hester said, "Thank you for saving me."

"Faro is a pig," said Kate.

"Yes," said Hester and to her shame, started to cry. "My brother and sister are at Sheriff Lawson's," she sobbed. "My other brother is working for John Hutchins; he is only twelve."

Coffee Kate slapped the reins and the oxen moved forward. She handed Hester

another tankard of coffee and took one herself. The cart rolled over hillocks and through brooks and upward into the dark depths of the woods. They arrived at a ramshackled cabin with a small corral attached. Kate unhitched the oxen and put them in the corral with hay, grain and water. Hester hobbled around as best she could, unloading the food and supplies. The cabin was small, but tidy. Kate started a fire and made coffee. There were two rocking chairs and a table. The sink had a pump and there were shelves and pegs. Soon they were settled and snug as two bugs in a rug.

Chapter Two (Six months later)

Hester had filled out and grown an inch. Her feet were covered with handmade rabbit skin boots and she had a buffalo cape over her. She stunk, but was so use to the smell of curing skins, she didn't notice. Over her head, she wore a hollowed out deer head so she appeared to have four eyes and horns. Kate wore the same smelly clothes day after day.

The had a large haul of skins and some especially fine white ermine and mink. They had muskrat, beaver, buffalo, deer, rabbit and one thick, black bearskin. The oxen were fat and bellowed at being put to work after a long winter of eating and relaxing.

"We go to fort first," said Kate, "sell goods and then to town."

Hester nodded. Neither woman talked much. Hester learned from Kate by example and she was proud she could trap, kill, skin and cure an animal almost as quickly as Kate. Hester had loved the quiet and solitude, but she was anxious to check on Zeke, Billy and Mary. And what about Faro? Would he still want her jailed?

Compared to the cool forest, the weather seemed hot and dry and dirty. The oxen were fractious with the heavy load.

Fort Flynn was built of brown pickets with a heavy gate guarded by four soldiers; two on each side.

"Hey, Coffee Kate," yelled a young guard. "I hope you got coffee for me. We've been looking for you."

"Ya," said Kate, "plenty of coffee.

The gates opened and Kate drove the oxen inside and to the supply store. A Frenchman named Big Jake ran the store and paid top dollar for skins which he sent east to St. Lois for profit. He was a very rich man. After examining the skins and haggling with Kate, they agreed on a price of two thousand dollars paid in gold dust. Hester was flabbergasted! All the aches and pains and cold and hard work faded away.

"We can camp at my old shack," said Hester, "if it's still standing."

Shortly after dark, they arrived at Hester's said looking shack. Weeds grew in the yard and the door hung off the hinges. Hester lit a fire and cooked food from this supplies. Kate fixed coffee.

"I see two ways to go," said Kate slowly. "I can ride into town, check it out, talk to the Sheriff, go to the bank, and come back to tell you; or we can both go and hope you don't get shot or arrested." It had been a long speech for her.

Hester didn't want to stay behind, but she didn't want to go to jail either.

"Can you check on Billy, Zeke and Mary?"

"Naw," said Kate, "Later." She rolled her saddle blanket out on the floor before the fire and was snoring in a few minutes.

Hester sat on the floor and nervously pondered how to proceed. Sometime during the night she fell asleep and when she woke, she was covered with Kate's saddle blanket, the fire was coals and Kate was gone.

Hester spent the day cleaning and repairing the sad little house. She gathered wood; repaired the door hinge; made a brush broom and swept the floor. She cooked stew and warmed some coffee. When she heard a horse whinny, she ran to the door. Kate was astride one of the oxen, leading a painted mare; followed by Sheriff Lawson on his chestnut.

The Sheriff nodded to Hester and led his horse to the trough for a drink. Kate winked at Hester and put her oxen away. The paint came to Hester who rubbed her nose and talked softly to her.

"I hope you belong to me," She whispered.

A draft wagon pulled by two horses drove into the yard. The driver frowned at Hester's rabbit boots, pants and shirt made out of skins. He unloaded boxes of pots, pans and bowls made of hollowed out wood; sacks of grain, flour, sugar and coffee.

Another wagon pulled up and two gruff men unloaded lumber, shingles, windows, barbed wire and barrels of nails and tools. When the wagons were unloaded, the men took shovels and began digging out the brook. Soon there was a large pond.

Kate kept tankards of coffee coming and the Sheriff sat on a rocking chair, drinking Kate's coffee and fanning himself with his Stetson.

"Billy is doing fine and seems happy at the farm. You can visit him. Betty Sue loves Mary. We are blessed to have her."

He paused and Hester got a bad feeling.

"A family came through town name of Barrows, going north. Seemed like a nice family and they took Zeke with them. They said they'd write when they settled, but have never heard."

"He's gone?"

" Afraid so," said the Sheriff regretfully. He didn't look at Hester.

The Sheriff sipped his coffee and cleared his throat. "No charges against you. Faro left town with the dance hall dolly and ain't no one heard from him again."

He rose and mounted his horse, riding away slowly without saying another word. Hester looked sadly after him. He had been her friend.

Chapter Three (Billy's rescue)

Kate and Hester rose slowly, savoring the clear morning air, and headed towards the Hutchins farm. They saw Billy in the field. He was hoeing. John Hutchins sat on the porch and Kate rode up to him and dismounted. Hester rode into the field and leaning over, she hugged Billy. She walked alongside of him, talking about the pelts and Kate and all she had learned. She told him how they had fixed up the cabin and that he might not recognize it. "Maybe you can visit," she suggested. Billy was quiet. He was sad when she mentioned Zeke and he asked about Mary. "Something's wrong," thought Hester.

Finally, she left him in the field telling him she would be

back soon. He half waved and continued down the long

row.

When Hester got to the house, she saw Kate on her

ox and no one else around.

"Not very friendly, are they?" Hester said.

Kate made a grumpy growl and they headed home.

Two days later, at Kate's insistence, the two women

visited Billy again. He was cleaning out the stalls and

dumping the dung in a huge pile behind the barn. Hester

thought he was very thin and looked unhappy. His clothes

were too small and were tattered. Mrs. Hutchins sat on the

porch shelling peas. "Mr. Hutchins went to town," she

said. She didn't offer any more information.

"Billy needs new clothes," Hester said.

Mrs. Hutchins rose and went inside.

Hester and Kate went to town and while Hester visited Mary, who was dressed in a beautiful lacy violet gown and playing with her rag doll, Kate went to the bank. Mary didn't seem too happy to see Hester, but shyly showed her a miniature tea set. Betty Sue was not friendly, but didn't stop Hester from visiting.

Three days later, Kate again insisted they visit Billy.

"Something ain't right," she told Hester.

The rode up slow and saw Billy picking corn. Kate rode up to Billy and reached down and ripped his shirt off his body. Hester gasped.

Billy's back was covered with criss-cross welts, some old, some new with dried blood festering in sores.

"Get on," growled Kate and lifted a squirming Billing onto the ox.

"No," yelled Bill, "No, he'll get mad.

Kate held onto him and rode to the cabin. Both man and woman came out of the house The woman had a black eye and a bloody cut on her forehead.

"He's leaving," Kate said.

"Get down Billy," yelled Mr. Hutchins. "You owe me for taking you on."

 Kate rode the ox right at Mr. Hutchins and if he hadn't moved, she would have mowed him down. They headed for town and rode to the Sheriff's Office where the Sheriff and Petey were drinking coffee. They looked up in surprise when Kate banged the door open. Kate turned Bill around, exposing the condition of Billy's back. The two men gasped.

"If Mr. Hutchins comes looking for Billy," Kate said meanly, "I will swear out a complaint against him.

Billy will be with us."

"Go to the stable and get a horse," she ordered Billy and gave Hester money. Kate went to the general store and bought clothes for him.

The three rode home quietly and that evening they made a bomb fire. They burned Billy's old clothes.

Chapter Three (Return to trapping)

Kate, Billy, and Hester worked ferociously building corrals; enlarging the cabin; shingling the roof; stuffing pallets and gathering supplies for the trip to the Trapping Cabin. Billy filled out and grew taller, but he never seemed really happy.

One evening as they sat on the porch drinking coffee, Billy said, "What if Pa comes back? He could take all this away."

They made a last trip to town and Hester and Billy visited Mary. They explained they would not be back until spring and Hester left a twenty dollar gold piece on the table. Kate hired an old, grizzled, ex-prospector named Jimmy Jack, to live in the cabin during the winter.

Kate gave Hester some papers. "I fixed it with the bank. You and Billy own the cabin and land."

Hester was happy to be back at the cabin in the

woods. Billy worked by their side, trapping and skinning and learning the skills. Soon he smelled as badly as the two women, but none of them noticed.

Billy shot a moose and he and Hester were skinning it when Kate appeared.

"Come," she said.

The put on snowshoes and tramped behind Kate. They knew if was no use to ask Kate where they were going. Kate had her own way of doing things. As they topped a knoll, they heard hooves muffled by the snow; lots of hooves.

Below, running fast and kicking up snow, were wild mustangs of every shape, color, age and size. The leader, a large brown stud, nipped and pushed his mares.

The three trappers watched them until they were out of sight.

"Golly," said Billy, "there must be a hundred horses. I betcha I could sell them to the Army at the fort."

"Clever," said Kate, "but who would break them?"

They returned to the cabin, each deep in thought.

Winter finally stopped and spring came running. Reluctantly they loaded the cart with pelts and furs and headed for the fort to sell their precious cargo.

Billy talked and gossiped all the way home repeating the news he had gleaned from the soldiers. He told the two women the Army would buy horses and they should go get some mustangs.

"The hard part will be breaking them," said Kate.

Chapter Four (Breaking Horses)

A week later, the three tired, but rich and satisfied trio, were on the porch drinking the ever-present coffee.

"Riders coming," said Kate. A small platoon of soldiers rode into the yard and the Captain introduced himself while his men watered their horses. Kate and Billy got out the coffee: Kate always believed her coffee solved all problems.

The Captain asked if they had horses for sale, explaining they must be well broke. The Army would pay twenty dollars gold per head.

Kate refilled his cup and aid "We can have them here one month from today."

Hester's mouth dropped open.

"Deal," said the Captain. "We'll be back in a

month."

After the soldiers mounted and rode away, Hester turned on Kate.

"And where do you think we will get horses?" she yelled. She stomped off to bed.

Kate went to town the next day and hired five cowboys for a roundup, telling them to meet her in two days at the ranch.

Billy and Hester scrambled around preparing to leave, gathering supplies, harvesting the garden and loading pack mules that Kate had bought in town. When the horse breakers arrived, there were only four, as one had taken a job elsewhere.

They rode hard and fast. Hester knew the men joked about her riding astride and wearing men's pants. They were easier with Kate because they loved the coffee.

Billy worked as their scout and it wasn't long before he located a herd of wild mustangs. It wasn't the same stud master; this one was white with a black tail.

The men located a dead end canyon and drove the horses in while Hester, Kate and Billy blocked the entrance with cactus and brush. Then came the back breaking work of busting broncos. Surprisingly Billy turned out to be the best and three weeks later, they counted sixty-four horses. They divided them into strings with each person leading a string. They traveled fast to the ranch; the men looked forward to their money and freedom. Jimmy Jack heard them coming and opened the corral.

The Captain and his men arrived on time and after checking each horse, took all but three. The three mares were with foal.

The men were paid and as they were riding away, one of the wranglers yelled, "Hey Hoss Woman, I'll ride with you any time."

Billy grabbed the name and referred to his sister as Hoss Woman from then on. Kate followed suit. The name Hester was lost in the dust of a mustang herd.

Chapter Four (Recruiting Women)

As summer flew by they discussed whether to go trapping or not. Kate wanted to go trap for one more year to increase their nest egg. Hoss Woman wanted to do another horse run and enlarge the ranch; and save more mares than the three having colts. Billy fluctuated between the women, not being able to agree with either one. They finally agreed to trap one more year and asked

Jimmy Jack if he would stay on and continue to care for the animals.

"Women are more reliable," offered Billy.

Kate mulled this over and on the trip, she and Hoss Woman discussed how they could recruit women to help at the ranch.

"Women who don't marry, end up as dance hall doilies or whores," said Hoss Woman. "We could advertise in a newspaper, train them and free them at the same time."

Kate nodded and Billy asked, "Where will they live?"

"Bunkhouse," said Kate. "Billy, build a bunkhouse."

It was a hard winter with heavy snow causing the animals to bury deep and hide. Time and time again the traps were empty. The wet snow caused snowshoes to jam up. Spring was slow in coming and their supplies were low. Their take was only half as much as the year before and they were depressed. The three trappers packed up their gear, cleaned the cabin, knowing they might never return.

They saws herds of mustangs in the distance.

Billy whistled, "I wish we could take them,"

Hoss Woman looked wistfully at the huge herd.

"Lots of money on the hooves," muttered Kate.

They made their usual stop at the fort, where they ate, sold furs at a reduced price and joked with the soldiers.

Hoss Woman and Billy went to check on their siblings who were not home. Kate went to the bank, ordered supplies at the store and joined her partners for the ride home.

Jimmy Jack greeted them: "I knew you'd be home soon; been watching." His grizzled face let up and he spit a wad of tobacco ten feed. Some chickens were scratching near the barn.

"Your neighbor came by and traded them chicks for four and coffee. Said her husband got kilt by a falling barrel. She had these two skinny young'uns with her. The Sheriff went east to visit family and left Petey in charge. Man named Snitch bought the saloon. You gels sure stink. Ain't no smell worse than trappers." Jimmy Jack spit a wad and stomped off on his short, bowed legs.

The trio discussed how to recruit women workers. They left Kate to hire men to build a bunkhouse and Billy and Hoss Woman rode to surrounding towns, putting ads in newspapers or hanging posters for women wranglers, horse breakers, farm workers, cooks and seamstresses.

On the way home they stopped at their neighbor's house where a woman was frying biscuits and beans on a campfire. Two children were hoeing in the garden.

After introductions, Billy said, "I hear you sew real good. We need new clothes and willing to pay you." The woman nodded. Hoss Woman took some apples out of saddlebag and left them for the children.

"She looks sad," Billy said on the way home.

Kate had the bunkhouse built and instead of one big crowded room, she had the men build ten rooms connected and opening on the porch running the length of the building. There were outhouses in the back. Each room had front and back doors, a window and a platform to sleep on. The men were working on a large kitchen complete with fireplace, sleeping loft and a small room attached for the cook.

"Do we have a cook? Can Jimmy Jack cook?" Billy asked.

Kate wrinkled her nose.

"Our neighbor can cook," said Hoss Woman.

When they all adjoined on the porch that evening for after dinner coffee, Jimmy Jack told them that the bank was taking their neighbor's house.

The next day, Kate and Hoss Woman left Billy and Jimmy Jack at the cabin and drove a small cart to their neighbor's house. She was cooking coffee over a fire in the yard.

"Would you like to help us out?" said Hoss Woman, putting her arm around the thin woman's shoulder.

"What's your name?" asked Kate.

"Beatrice," she answered softly.

"We need a cook and a seamstress. We would like to buy your house and land and give you and the children a place to live; food; and work. We would pay off the bank and take the house," Hoss Woman continued.

Beatrice poked at the fire.

"Could the children go to school? I've always wanted Joshua and Grace to read and figure."

Kate said, "I teach Billy in the evening and I could teach yours as well."

Hoss Woman directed the children to empty the cart of the foodstuff they had brought. She handed each a peppermint stick.

"I'll let you know," said Beatrice sadly.

On the way home, Kate said, "Don't have much choice does she?"

Kate, Hoss Woman, Billy and Jimmy Jack worked the rest of the day to the sound of the man expanding the corrals and barn.

One of the mares, a cute little appaloosa was restless and whinnied every few minutes.

"She'll foal before morning," predicted Jimmy Jack. He was right.

After supper they sat on the porch sipping Coffee Kate's famous coffee and down the road came Beatrice and her two children trailing behind.

"Welcome," said Kate and handed them all coffee.

"That's good," Beatrice said beaming.

Hoss Woman thought, "Our family is growing. She thought wistfully of Zeke and Mary, lost to her, probably forever.

Chapter Six (Growth and expansion)

Beatrice fit in quickly and nicely. The children

Joshua, 12, and Grace, 10, were filling out, growing taller

and laughing. They adored Billy and followed him

around.

There were three new foals in the corral and Hoss

Woman often paused to feed them carrots or apples and

pat them.

Hoss Woman and Billy went to town to Feathers General Store for supplies and he seemed friendlier than usual.

"Humph," thought Hoss Woman. "We bring him lots of business."

"Mr. Feathers," she said politely, "How does one advertise for help? Women who need a nice place to live and work for good wages?"

"I'll ask around," he answered.

"And how do I mail a letter?"

"Leave it here and I put in on the stage. Two pennies a page."

"Has the Sheriff returned?"

"Nope,"

Hoss Woman added a dozen licorice sticks to her

order.

She and Billy went to the bank and asked to see Mr. Barrows, the manager. He was a portly gentleman with a bald head, wearing a three piece suit and a pocket watch in his vest.

"I'm a busy man," he said rudely. "What do you want?"

Hoss Woman looked past him and saw the teller smirk.

"I'm Hester Harmon and this is my brother Billy. May we talk to you in private?"

"I know who you are and how you took advantage of my daughter and her husband, the Sheriff, by pawning off your brat on them. I'm a busy man; too busy to see the likes of you."

"Coffee Kate and I want to buy the neighboring

ranch."

"I don't loan to women," he said nastily.

"We don't want a loan. We'll buy the place cash on the barrel head."

"Five hundred dollars," he said.

"No," said Hoss Woman, "two hundred fifty. They owe you two hundred and that will give you fifty dollars profit." Her voice was loud.

The few patrons of the bank had stopped and were listening intently. Hoss Woman knew the conversation would be all over town lickety-split.

Mr. Barrows noticed the attention and turned beet red.

"Where are you going to get cash?" he demanded.

"None of your affair," Hoss Woman announced

angrily, "but it is from honest labor. If you want to sell, draw up the papers; bring them to our ranch tomorrow; the money will be waiting."

Billy and Hoss Woman left for home. Hoss Woman noticed that Billy clothes were tight and he would soon need more; he was almost a grown man. Hoss Woman made a mental note to buy a shaving kit from Mr. Feathers.

Mr. Barrows didn't arrive until late afternoon and Kate had been muttering that she might have to go to town to give him a piece of mind. He drank some of her coffee and smacked his lips and handed over the papers.

"Can I have the recipe?" he asked as so many other before had asked.

"Only Kate knows and she ain't sharing with anyone," Billy said.

Kate read each page carefully and slowly, licking her fingers as she turned a page.

Mr. Barrows was growing impatient.

"I can read it to you," he said nastily.

Kate ignored him and Billy snickered which earned him a stern glance from his sister. Beatrice smiled. Kate nodded and the three women and Billy signed the deeds and contracts. Mr. Barrows placed the papers and money in his case and was soon out of sight.

"Travelers," said Kate and everyone turned to the road. Two women stood on the other side of the creek. Their attire proclaimed them loose women.

Nervously, they approached.

Kate served coffee (as usual) and Beatrice brought bowls of stew and biscuits which they ate hungrily.

Mae Betts and Sarah Turner were friends and had

seen Hoss Woman's ad in the paper.

"I ain't happy servicing cowboys," Mae said. She had large brown eyes and bowed lips. She looked Hoss Woman in the eyes as she spoke. "Me Pa threw me out a few years back. I tried to get honest work. The Sheriff found me sleeping in an alley and let me sleep in the jail for a while. The saloon owner, Faro, came by and offered me a job."

Kate and Hoss Woman exchanged looks.

"I wanted you to know," Mae said defensively. "Sarah," nodding at her companion, "was already working upstairs and serving drinks downstairs. Sometimes she sang; she was a right pretty voice."

Hoss Woman introduced everyone and said she was tired. She told Billy and Joshua to show the women to their rooms.

"Mae's pretty," said Billy.

"Sort of," said Joshua.

The next day Beatrice set the girls to work helping her cook, clean and weed the garden. Beatrice cut out new pants and shirts and started sewing. Mae and Sarah helped her and soon the clothes were finished as they giggled and gossiped.

Hoss Woman banged open the door and yelled, "Ain't we eating today? I thought you had all run off."

The girls jumped and looked wild eyed, but Beatrice laughed. "I might feed you if you go bath in the pond and put on new clothes. You smell like an old randy sheep."

Everyone went in the water and Kate even came up with a precious sliver of soap. The guys giggled and splashed and turned red at the sight of near-naked women. Jimmy Jack mumbled curses about the evils of water and 'nekkid' women tempting men to evil ways. Mae and Sarah captured him and threw him in clothes and all. He came up sputtering, but everyone knew he was pleased with the attention.

Mae and Sarah were uncomfortable in pants and kept pulling on them. They drank the coffee and gossiped.

"Can you ride?" asked Billy.

Mae said no and Sarah said yes. Billy bought out a saddled horse and boosted Sarah on. She rode astride and did well. Everyone clapped when she dismounted, so she took a bow.

Billy showed Mae how to mount and led her around the yard. She clutched the saddle horn. Billy soon had her riding by herself.

Jimmy Jack came by for coffee and asked Kate, "When are you leaving?"

Kate said, "Two days." and Jimmy Jack returned to the barn.

Beatrice asked, "Where are you going?"

"Billy, Kate, and me are going to round up mustangs and bring them back to break them. We'll sell them to the Army." Hoss Woman said. We're leaving you and Sarah, Mae, Joshua, Grace and Jimmy John to do the work."

Billy said, "I think Joshua should come with us. We can use one more hand."

Joshua begged and pleaded until his mother relented and early morning found a happy, noisy group riding out. It wasn't long before Billy, acting as their scout, came racing back to tell them he had located a herd. Thus began the long, dusty trail back to the ranch. The herders whistled and sang and urged the mares in the right direction. Joshua learned that the stud was the trick to keeping the mares moving. No one stopped; they slept in their saddles; eating beef jerky and hard tack. Some of the mares escaped, but most of them stayed with the herd, scared and nervous.

When the ranch came in sight, Jimmy Jack opened the corrals and they drove the mares inside before the herd realized there was no exit. After pitchforking lots of hay and putting grain in the buckets and filling water barrels, they went to eat.

"Now comes the hard work," exclaimed Billy.

At dawn, Hoss Woman and Jimmy Jack fastened rope halters and put them on the nearest horses. They snorted and wheeled around the corral. They separated the haltered ones.

Billy, Joshua, Mae and Sarah filled grain sacks with

sand, tied two together and threw them over a haltered horse. They bucked and kicked but in the end the heavy weight of the sand took its toll and they stood, shivering.

They repeated the procedure with another set of horses, culling out any mares who were with foal. The stud was furious about his ladies and whinnied and reared and raced around. They weren't sure if they should geld him and keep him or turn him back to the wild.

After several hours they took the grain sacks off a horse and replaced them with a saddle. Then the riding began. Billy rode three mares without being bucked off, but the fourth was a tough little mare who sent him flying. The hot, dirty work went on all day and into the evening with Billy and Hoss Woman taking turns. Coffee Kate's drink tasted extra good that evening. Hoss Woman was sure that every muscle in her body was broken.

"Traveler," said Kate.

Everyone looked to the road and saw a tall, thin woman with a pork chop hat on her head leaning on a cane. She walked up to the porch. She wore small glasses perched on the end of her nose.

"Hoss Woman?" she asked.

Everyone pointed at her.

"Minora Brown," she said, extending her hand. "Late school teacher who is now unemployed. I am here to answer your ad."

Kate handed her coffee and she sipped slowly.

"Delicious," she said.

Billy and Josh showed her to a room.

"Eight rooms to go," said Kate. And they all went to bed.

Chapter Seven (The Fort)

The next few weeks were a blur of hot work, painful falls, scrapes, rope burns, cuts and bruises. Billy and Hoss Woman took the brunt of busting broncos, but Joshua did his share, as well as Mae and Sarah, by leading horses around, lugging saddles, making halters, lead ropes and grain sacks.

Minora and Beatrice sewed and cooked and tended the garden, chicks, pigs and goats. Kate made coffee, hauled water, cleaned, washed clothes and helped Jimmy Jack pitch hay and grain and lug water.

Everyone was exhausted at the end of two weeks, but satisfied with jobs well done.

"Day off tomorrow," announced Kate and everyone cheered.

"Billy and I are riding to the fort to sell horses," Hoss Woman announced.

"Can I go?" asked Joshua.

"Me, too," said Mae.

"I wanna go," said Sarah.

Kate suggested they rest a day and all go the day

after. Minora, Beatrice and Jimmy John agreed to stay behind. Grace said she would stay with her ma.

The six friends left early and were greeted exuberantly by the soldiers. It was a pleasure to shop at Big Jake's store instead of Feathers General Store. Kate and Hoss woman stocked up on supplies and bought two milk cows.

"Hey Hoss Woman," yelled a young soldier across the Parade Ground, "Gonna stay for the dance. I wanna be first."

Hoss Woman smiled and Kate grunted. Sarah giggled and yelled back, "I'm available for your friend."

After dinner with the Captain where there was too much drink and they ate tasteless Army food, everyone assembled on the Parade Ground. The fiddler and harmonica player tuned up; the soldiers took turns with the ladies. Billy was jealous that Mae was so popular and sulked on the sidelines, drinking too much. He would regret the next day. Joshua danced with everyone and then retired to drink with Billy, another sorry character with a hangover the next day.

When Hoss Woman rose the next morning, she caught Billy and Mae sneaking out of the grain storage shed.

Hoss Woman smiled and acted as though she hadn't seen them.

Kate served coffee and everyone was rounded up to begin the trip home.

The Captain ordered soldiers to mount up and ordered a wagon with supplies and tents. When they arrived at the ranch, the soldier pitched their tents across the stream, built fires and cooked.

Captain Thomas came to the bunkhouse and ate with everyone else. He sat on the porch drinking coffee.

The next day was gray and threatening rain. The soldiers broke camp; rounded up the horses; stringing them together to lead to the fort.

Captain Thomas paid Kate, thanked everyone and mounted. He hesitated and leaned down grabbing the back of Hoss Woman's neck and kissed her soundly.

One of the soldiers whistled, another gave a rebel yell, and a third yelled, "Hey Cap, you wife ain't gonna like that."

Captain and Hoss Woman both froze. The Captain moved first and looking straight ahead, gave the command to move forward. The Captain never looked back.

Chapter Seven (The Smithy and the Preacher Man)

The Sheriff returned and Billy took Mae into town

to meet Mary.

When they returned, Billy reported that Mary was a

lovely young lady who seemed happy to see him. She sent

her regards to their sister.

"The bad news is that Mr. Feathers has raised all his

prices. We need our own store."

The small band of coffee drinkers heard a loud

voice singing and a strange sight appeared. Four large mules were pulling a loaded black wagon and sitting high holding four reins and bellowing was a giant of a man with black curly hair and smiling blue eyes. He hopped down and bowed.

"Do I have the honor of addressing Hoss Woman?" he said with an Irish lilt in his voice. "Shamus O'Shaughnessy at your service; blacksmith extraordinaire; anything metal you need, I can make it. A right handy gent, am I."

Kate smiled and said "Sit yourself down Shamus and have some of the best coffee in the world. They call me Coffee Kate."

"Well, Katie, my darling," said Shamus, "any cup from your hand would be ambrosia."

The group stared with open mouths until Hoss

Woman rose and introduced herself. She held out her hand which Shamus turned over and kissed, making her blush.

Everyone stayed up late listening to the Irish blarney Shamus told and singing songs. He had a loud, but pretty baritone which everyone enjoyed.

Kate and Shamus stayed up long after the rest had gone to bed and in the morning Kate told them all at breakfast that they were building a store with a smith attached. She showed them plans and sent Billy and Hoss Woman to town to order lumber and hire carpenters.

They visited with Mary, ordered the lumber, hired workers, telling them they could stay in the bunkhouse until the work was done.

Shamus set up his smith outdoors and made new pots and metal forks and spoons. The four large jacks were put in the corral. Every evening Kate and Shamus went for a walk, holding hands and everyone smiled when they heard Shamus singing love songs.

Hoss Woman and Billy made lists of what to buy to supply the store. They all had different ideas and different lists so they combined them.

"I think Billy and Joshua should go to St. Louis to fill the orders," said Hoss Woman. "If they left right away, they would be back in time for the smith and store to open for business.

Beatrice frowned. "I think Joshua is too young for such a long trip."

Minora said, "Pshaw, he's almost a grown man and he needs to get out from under your apron strings."

"I want to go," pouted pretty Mae, "I want to see St. Louis." Everyone ignored her.

The siblings went to town to see Mary. They tied

their horses in front of the Sheriff's Office and were

entering when an Army patrol came into town led by

Captain Thomas. When he saw Hoss Woman he called a

halt and dismounted, calling her name.

"Stay away from me," Hoss Woman hissed with

such venom the Captain stepped back and turned red.

Billy stepped forward in a protective manner.

Hoss Woman was surprised that Billy was taller

than she was and he had fuzz on his face and his hair was

long.

"Let's go to the barber," Hoss Woman suggested.

Billy shuffled his feet and avoided eye contact. "I'm

out of money," he mumbled. "Mae hides it all away for the

future."

"You need to marry," his sister snapped.

"No preacher and no church," Billy snapped back.

Hoss Woman paid the barber and said, "If you hear anyone wanting a job, send her our way. Room, board and good wages." The barber's eyebrows rose at "her" but nodded.

Billy and Hoss Woman spent some time with Mary and left two twenty dollar gold pieces on the table. It was dark when the arrived home. They all complimented Bill on his haircut and Jimmy Jack said it was so nice that he might get one – some day.

Shamus, Kate and Hoss Woman stayed later than the others and Hoss Woman told them Billy and Mae would marry if there was a preacher. "Maybe others want to get married too," she added pointedly.

"Shall we put an ad in the paper for a preacher? Build a school and a rectory? Minora wants a school and a library."

"Money running out," said Kate.

"Saw the Captain in town. Maybe he won't buy horses from us anymore."

"Traveler," said Kate.

"Hello the house," said a man riding up on a beautiful palomino. His tack was fancy, studded with silver and turquoise, as were his jacket and pants. He wore a flat, black hat with silver trim.

"Hello," said Hoss Woman, "Come, sit and have the world's best coffee made by Coffee Kate. This is our smithy, Shamus and I'm Hoss Woman.

"I am Henry and this is Harvey," he said. Harvey bowed low.

They clapped. "Let me see to Harvey first," Henry said.

"I'll do it," said Jimmy Jack coming out of the barn.

"Come on my beauty; nice oats, plenty of water; good hay," and he led Harvey away.

"Rub her down good," called Henry and joined them on the porch, smacking his   lips after drinking Kate's coffee.

Minora called from the bunkhouse, "If you want supper, it's on the back of the stove," and she disappeared back into the bunkhouse.

"I am looking for some good horses," Henry said, "and the soldiers at Fort Flynn told me this is the best place to come. I plan on settling near here. I have some long horns coming from Texas."

"You came to the right place," said Hoss Woman. "How many?"

"Depends on the price," Henry said shrewdly.

"Let's talk tomorrow," said Kate. "Show him to the

bunkhouse." She and Shamus went for their walk.

Henry was taller than Hoss Woman and wore silver spurs that jingled. His face was tanned and while he was not as handsome as Captain Thomas, he was nice and an easy companion. He ate a meal in the kitchen while he discussed cattle and horses. By the time she showed him to his room, she was yawning and sleepy and stumbled home.

Kate came to Hoss Woman next morning and said, "Let's take Henry to Beatrice's farm and we can get rid of it. It's too far for us to use and to close to sell to just anyone."

"Good idea," said Hoss Woman.

Afer assigned chores to the others, Hoss Woman and Henry rode over to Beatrice's farm. Henry told her he always wanted to come west, but his wife wouldn't leave their home town and she had bought a lot of money to the

marriage, so he went along with her.

"It was a comfortable marriage," he continued, "But

after she passed all those longings to move west plagued

me and I finally gave in to it. I like to train horses for fun.

Harvey is my best results. I bought some cows and bulls

and decided to specialize in meat cattle, so I here I am

looking for a new home.

They arrived at the farm and Henry walked through

the barn the house, the shed, the corrals and drank from

the brook.

"Originally," said Hoss Woman, a man named

Barrows owned five hundred acres. He runs the bank

now. He split the land into two parcels, selling one to

Bernice's husband and one to my Pa."

"Is there two hundred fifty acres of pasture?"

"No," she said, "I think about half are pasture but the rest could be cleared. We've cleared about a hundred acres of our ranch."

When they returned, they ate supper and gathered for Coffee Kate's special drink.

Henry asked, "What are you asking for the ranch?"

Beatrice answered, "My husband paid one thousand dollars for the land fifteen years ago and together we built all the improvements. We could never make enough to live on so my husband ran a freight business. After he died, I sold it to Kate and Hoss Woman and moved here."

Kate said, "Mr. Barrows could tell you what he thinks it's worth."

Henry said, "Maybe I'll go to the bank tomorrow and see what he says."

"Pardon," said the foreman of the carpenters. "We

have finished the smithy and store and would like you to examine them before we leave."

They all walked to the new buildings and "o-o-o-oh" and "o-o-o" over the workmanship. The workmen wanted to go home so Kate and Hoss Woman paid them and asked them to return when the supplies arrived from St. Louis to build the church and rectory. They nodded.

After visiting with Mr. Barrows at the bank, Henry offered twenty-five hundred dollars for the ranch, but Kate and Hoss Woman asked for three thousand and Henry agreed. They hired Lawyer Gilchrist to prepare the papers and they would be ready in a week.

Hoss Woman mailed ads to several newspapers for a reverend.

Jimmy Jack reported that all the mares had been covered by the stud. They were not sure what to do with the magnificent beast.

Shamus was getting business from town and the anvil range most all day and sometimes into the early evening. The garden was ready for harvest and the women discussed the best way to preserve the vegetables.

"Neither of you have been to town since your moved here," Kate said to the women, "Would you like to pick up our supplies and do errands for us?"

The women were happy to oblige and early the next day Minora, Beatrice and Grace set off in the buckboard in high spirits.

"Did you hear gun shots yesterday?" asked Shamus. "I think I'll ride over to visit Henry and see what he says about it."

The ladies returned and Shamus arrived with Henry. No one knew who was shooting. After dinner, Shamus serenaded them in his beautiful baritone and Henry played

a harmonica. It began to rain so Henry spent the night and

everyone retired.

The days passed busy and happy except for Mae

who pined for Billy.

"Those boys are taking their time," complained

Beatrice worriedly.

"They will be along any day now," said Hoss

Woman.

Henry's cattle arrive with swirling dust and weary

drovers yipping and whistling. Everyone rode over to see

the Texas longhorns and admire them. Hoss Woman

invited the weary cowboys to dinner and they accepted.

Henry had build a bunkhouse with a great room for

cooking and eating and three rooms to each side.

"I liked your idea of single rooms so much, I copied

your idea. Now I need a cook."

Hoss Woman explained how she advertised and Henry thought she was clever.

"Will you give her your coffee recipe?" Henry asked Kate.

Every laughed since they all knew Kate would never ever give it to anyone; not even her beloved Shamus.

"I need horses," said Henry.

"It's time for us to go on a round up," said Kate and everyone agreed.

Arriving home, they saw a large freight wagon with two drivers and a guard along with weary and dirty Joshua and Billy. They directed them to the store and the men unloaded everything in the storeroom to be sorted out later.. The men were invited to supper which they accepted and to spend the night, which they declined.

Billy and Joshua went swimming to wash off the road dirt and then everyone gathered on Hoss Woman's front porch for Kate's nightly coffee routine.

"Who's running the store?" asked Billy.

"I want to," said Grace shyly. Everyone turned in surprise to the young woman who seldom spoke, yet worked as hard as any of them.

"Good idea," they said in unison.

"We need a horse run," said Hoss Woman. "Who wants to go?"

Billy, Josh and Mae volunteered. Shamus and Kate decided to go and it was decided they would leave after a short rest.

Hoss Woman stood at the window of her room, looking out into the starry night, unable to sleep. Billy and Mae were together; Kate and Shamus were in love. Who was for her? She spied someone moving near the bunkhouse and identified Henry and Beatrice clinched in a passionate embrace which made Hoss Woman even more depressed.

Billy, Joshua, Mae, Sarah, Shamus and Kate left at dawn, Hoss Woman went to town to advertise the store and visit with Mary. She had grown tall and was dressed in a beautiful blue gown. She didn't say much to Hoss Woman and looked at her pants, boots and flannel shirt with distaste. Hoss Woman put two twenty dollar gold pieces on the table and left despondently. She thought of Zeke and hoped he was well cared for by loving people. Hoss Woman visited the newspaper office and put in ads to hire women and an announcement of the store's opening.

It was beautiful weather and she enjoyed a peaceful

ride back to the ranch. Jimmy Jack led the pretty little

mare away and then Minora joined them on the porch with

some cool lemonade.

"Wagon coming," said Jimmy Jack, "I hear the

wheel squeaking."

A man of color drove a small wagon drawn by a

beaten down shaggy pony and stopped at the porch. A

young man perched on the bench seat beside him.

"Howdy, Reverend Josiah Singleton at your

service," he said politely, doffing his dusty, worn cap.

"This is my son Simon," he added indicating the tall,

lanky handsome man of color sitting beside him. "We are

in need of a smithy as I am sure you heard."

"Come and sit," and Hoss Woman served them

lemonade. Grace came from the store and Beatrice from

the bunkhouse kitchen. After introductions were

complete, Jimmy Jack told them where the smithy had gone.

"Shamus won't mind if you use his tools," Jimmy Jack said and on the way to the the blacksmith shop, he said, "Where you headed?" Patting the pony on his nose he continued, "This little guy needs some rest and hay and oats."

Grace walked along quietly, returning to her store. Hoss Woman resumed her porch sitting and dozed off until the kitchen triangle rang for dinner.

Minora and Beatrice outdid themselves at dinner and after a hearty meal, lots of laughter and cleanup, everyone ended up on Hoss Woman's porch drinking warmed over coffee Kate had left. Grace and Simon played cat's cradle with string and Simon showed her some added moves. She wished Kate was here to help her decide if she should hire the Reverend for the church pulpit. Kate was a master at judging people sharply and quickly.

"Please show the Reverent and Simon to their rooms," she directed Grace. "I am tired." Everyone soon followed suit, each wondering if Hoss Woman would offer the Reverend work.

"Please stay a few days," Hoss Woman said at breakfast. "We can always use extra hands and your pony looks beat up."

The Reverend looked at Simon and they both nodded. They built another coral and the Reverend worked on his cart at the smithy. Simon helped Grace in the store. They all heard shots from the mountain between Henry's and Hoss Woman's ranches. Henry rode over for dinner and he and the Reverend were soon in deep conversation.

Three days later, Hoss Woman heard the yip, yip and whistle of the bronco busters, along with beating hooves. Everyone ran to open the corral gates wide and soon the connecting rings were full of snorting, neighing, running mares with one mad-as-a hornet stud.

The dusty, tired crew threw off most of their clothes and jumped into the pond to cool down and clean up.

Kate and Shamus stood beside Hos Woman with big smiles.

"Big haul," Kate said.

"Beautiful," said Hoss Woman. "Even the new corral isn't quite enough. We have to keep those studs separated or we will have a terrible fight. Maybe Henry will want one of them or we can geld him."

Shamus asked, "Who are the dark men?"

"Reverend Josiah Singleton and his son Simon," said Hoss Woman. "Just resting a few days on their way west."

"Can he marry us?" asked Shamus. Kate blushed. "A wedding or two: that would be just the thing."

"Mae's with child," said Kate.

"No surprise," said Hoss Woman. "Those two are like rabbits. Better have Billy talk to the Reverend too."

"Me too," said Kate shyly.

Hoss Woman was shocked. Kate had never seemed the motherly type, but then Hoss Woman remembered the way Kate had nursed her and kept her safe. She grasped Kate's hand and aid, "I'm so happy for you. This calls for a special celebration." The two women hugged. Billy and Shamus were shaking hands with Josiah and grinning ear to ear.

There were lots of plans to be made and everyone contributed their ideas.

They built two more corrals and made rope halters and grain sacks full of sand and started the long, hot, painful process of busting the broncos.

Hoss Woman didn't get thrown at all and Billy only once. They grinned at each other and slapped hands. They were getting good at this. Late in the afternoon, Hoss Woman was saddling a contentious black and white mare and saw the Sheriff leaning on the fence watching her. She wondered what he wanted after such a long time. Dust rose around her choking her and covering her with a fine alkaline film. The mare was a nasty piece of work and it took a long time to settle her.

As soon as the dinner bill rang, Hoss Woman nodded at the Sheriff and walked straight into the refreshing, cool pond. A weary, wet woman ate what was put in front of her, too tired to taste anything.

"Shamus says he hears rifle shots on the hill," said the Sheriff. "Henry has heard them too and his cowhands think someone is living in a cave up there. You know anything?"

Hoss Woman shook her head and the Sheriff headed back to town taking wedding notices and church services notices to the newspaper inviting everyone to the celebrations.

On Sunday, the Reverend preached a short sermon and Shamus sang in his beautiful voice. Simon sang and his voice was soothing, the hymn soaring into the blue sky to honor the day.

They had gathered on the porch when the Captain and his troopers rode up. The Captain dismounted and walked up to Hoss Woman and kissed her thoroughly in front of all. Joshua and Billy whistled and Simon whooped. Hoss Woman blushed. Kate got more coffee. Shamus introduced the Reverend and his son Simon. The weary ranchers wandered off and the Reverend walked over to the encampment and spent time talking to the troops.

"Two weeks to the weddings. Horses will be ready by then."

The Captain nodded. "We'll be here."

Hoss Woman broke broncos all day, alternating with Joshua and Billy. Everyone helped with the chores. Shamus worked the anvil; Simon and Grace worked in the store; Sarah and Mae sewed wedding gowns and trousseaus. Minora and Beatrice cooked, cleaned, milked the cows; tended the garden, chicks and hogs.

Henry came over and liked the stud so much, he paid the asking price with haggling. Two of his cowboys led the handsome male away kicking and screaming all the way.

Hoss Woman was tired and sore, but oh, so content. She hoped it would stay this way.

Chapter Eight (Zeke)

The weddings took place on a beautiful, sunny day, directly after Reverend Singleton preached a rousing sermon. Both brushing brides were pretty and both nervous grooms were sweating and shaking. It was exciting.

A fiddler tuned up and the hard cider flowed. They

toasted the happy couples and danced most of the night. They consumed tons of food and everyone was friendly. Even Jimmy Jack danced and the soldiers grabbed partners, both young and old alike.

The wagons and carts were sluggishly loaded and everyone sleepily called goodbyes and see y'all later.

The troopers broke camp and were busy tying the broke horses so they could be led to the fort. One small brown mare kicked up such a fuss, they cut her out and left her behind.

Late one afternoon, Deputy Petey rode up. He dismounted slowly as Hoss Woman came out of the chicken coop with a basket of eggs on her way to the kitchen.

"Come have coffee," she called and Petey sat at a table with a tankard. Kate and Shamus arrived, followed by Bill, Simon and Joshua. Minora and Beatrice were cooking but stayed in hearing distance.

Petey cleared his throat two or three times and said, "The Sheriff was shot this morning. The troopers brought him into the doc; looks like he was coming or going from here. You seen him?"

"How bad is he?" asked Kate. "He was at the weddings on Sunday with Mary and Betty Sue."

"Doc says he'll make it? Have you hear any more shots from the hill?"

"Once in a while," said Billy slowly, glancing at Joshua and Simon. "We think someone is living in a cave up there, but he's slicker than greased lightening. We tried to find him a few times, but no luck."

"I went by Henry's first," Petey continued. "His men said the same thing. Do you think it could be your brother Zeke?"

Hoss Woman looked surprised. Billy and Kate exchanged looks.

"Zeke!" Hoss Woman squealed.

"Mr. Feathers claims he saw a young man, maybe Zeke, stealing a chicken from his coop. Wouldn't Zeke contact you or Billy if he was around?"

"Zeke!" Hoss Woman repeated in amazement.

"Why would he –?" but she stopped. Would Zeke blame the Sheriff for sending him away?

"Well, keep you eyes peeled. If I led a posse, the town would be unprotected with the Sheriff laid up. Of course if the Sheriff dies, I won't have a choice."

"We can look for the person in the cave. I think we can find him," said Simon with the conviction of youth.

As Petey rode off, Shamus told the others, "Now that's a sorry piece of a man; wants us to do his work for him."

After dinner, the three young men saddled four horses and leading one, left for the the hill.

Hoss Woman wanted to go, but Billy firmly told her she was needed here. He asked Shamus to help Grace in the store lift some sacks for an order that had arrived yesterday.

Hoss Woman admired Bill's leadership and how he grasped what was needed around the ranch.

Two foals were born that night and were soon standing on wobbly, knobby knees – real beauties. Hoss Woman and Jimmy Jack examined the horses in the corrals and determined ther were two more ready for birth. Hoss Woman felt a thrill and was very proud.

"What a team we have," she said to Jimmy Jack, who smiled like a proud papa.

At their nightly coffee drinking, Hoss Woman noticed that both Mae and Kate wer showing with child.

"Our next generation," thought Hoss Woman with mixed feelings. "I hope I am part of it."

The building foreman appeared out of the dark and reported that the rectory was finished and he requested he be allowed to give his men a week off before starting the and library.

Hoss Woman nodded and the foreman tipped his hat. He was really happy to be working for these two strange birds who dressed as men. His crew was glad to be working here as well and the wages were good.

The three boys did not return that night.

Jimmy John called Hoss Woman to the barn and

they helped another foal into the world.

"That stud is sure busy," he muttered.

Hoss Woman and Kate went to town to check on the Sheriff and put a notice up that everyone was invited to the dedication of the new church to be followed by a picnic and social. Kate found the fiddler in the saloon and asked him to play at the gathering. Hoss Woman went to visit Mary, but no one was home so she met Kate at the doc's office as they had agreed.

Betty Sue and Mary were there.

"He's holding his own," said doc. "Any news on who done it?"

"I haven't heard," said Kate.

"Well, it was on your property," he exclaimed sourly.

Betty Sue and Mary didn't say anything to the two

women and Mary turned her back when Hoss Woman

tried to speak to her.

They left their notice at the newspaper office,

tightened their cinches and mounted to leave town when

Mr. Feathers stepped out of his store and hollered at them.

Mr. Smith came out of the barber shop to listen.

"Hoss Woman," he yelled, raising his fist, "you

think you can put me out of business by opening your own

store? You think you can shoot the Sheriff and get away

with it? You're going to pay, you are."

The Reverend appeared and stepped in front of Mr.

Feathers. "Peace brother," he said calmly. "Hoss Woman

didn't shoot anyone and friendly competition doesn't hurt

either of you. Threats are bad for business.

"What's going on here?" said Petey, coming from

his office.

"Nothing," said the Reverend. "We just having a neighborly chat."

No one said much on the way home, but they heard gunshot from the hill.

Minora ran out to greet them. "Mae's in labor."

Kate said, "too early" and went to help Minora and Beatrice.

Sarah took over the cooking and everyone was on edge.

`   After supper Hoss Woman and Grace sat on the porch drinking lemonade and speculating about the baby, the man in the cave, who may have shot the Sheriff, and how many people would come on Sunday for the church service, picnic and social. Hoss Woman told Grace about Mr. Feathers' tirade and warned her to be hyper vigilant when she was in the store. Shamus came by to sit for a while.

"If the boys ain't back tomorrow I'm gonna look for them," he said.

Hoss Woman was in bed but not asleep when she heard a horse coming fast. She dressed quickly and went outside. It was Billy.

"Saddle up," he called softly, "I have to show you something."

He stripped the saddle off his sweating mare and led out fresh horses. Hoss Woman was saddled when Jimmy Jack called sleepily, "What's up?"

"Nothing," said Bill, "just gotta show Hoss Woman something. Be back tomorrow."

"Wait, Mae went into labor. Kate and the other women are with her."

Billy took off running for the bunkhouse. Minora

met him at the door and they talked softly for a while before Billy came back.

"Minora says everything is gonna be all right. Let's go."

Billy led the way up the hill. The way was steep and rocky and the horses were skittish in the dark. When the sun started to show light in the east, the going got easier. Simon and Josh stood near the entrance of a cave, their horses tethered nearby.

When Hoss Woman entered the shallow cave, she hesitated a moment to adjust her eyesight. She saw a body lying on the rock floor tied up with a rope.

"Zeke," she cried, kneeling by his side. "Is this you Zeke?"

He turned her head.

"Hester," he whimpered. "My sister Hester." He

started to cry.

"Untie him immediately," Hoss Woman ordered. "Why did you truss him up like this?"

Billy knelt an undid the boy's arms and legs. He rubbed his arms and legs attempting to rejuvenate his circulation.

"What happened to you Zeke?" Hoss Woman asked.

The boy headed outside.

"Please Zeke," begged Horse Woman, "Don't leave. Whatever it is, we can fix it."

Zeke hesitated and turned back. His pants were torn and filthy. He had no shirt on and was barefoot. His feet were cut and scratched and blood had dried on them. His hair was long and his face was dirty.

"Why did you leave me?" he said sadly. "Why didn't you take me instead of Billy?"

Hoss Woman started talking slowly. All the boys gathered around as she told her sorry story. She started with Faro's advances and her escape with Coffee Kate's help. Each young man sat enthralled by her narrative, sometimes with tears in their eyes and sometimes laughing. Zeke moved closer and closer until he was hugging her.

"The Sheriff didn't want us," he began. "Betty Sue only wanted Mary, she didn't want boys, so Billy went to a farm and I was given to a man named Frederick Baker, his wife Faith and two little girls, Eliza and Lottie. We traveled north as he had told the Sheriff he would, and we headed into Wyoming Territory. Frederick would hit anyone who didn't obey immediately. I tried to run away and come back, but he tied me to the wagon wheel. We didn't have much food." He stopped and heaved a sign. He swallowed hard and continued. "When we got to

Wyoming, he filed for a homestead on twenty acres. He bought a bullwhip and would whop us when we didn't do the work to his satisfaction. He kept everything locked up and took out only what he wanted us to eat. We were always hungry. One day he took Faith, Lottie and me to remove rocks from the field to make room for crops. It was hard going and we only got water at noon. Frederick sat under a tree and threatened us often as he usually did When the sun went down, he took us back to the sod shack. Eliza had cooked, but then she had eaten most of it and was asleep. Poor little thing had been so hungry. Frederick went crazy. He kicked her and beat her and wouldn't stop. When Faith and Lottie and I begged him to quit, he hit us too.." Zeke stopped and started to sob on Hoss Woman's shoulder. "He killed her," he whispered.

"He killed that poor little girl because she was hungry. Faith told Lottie and I to dig a grave and we went outside but we didn't dig the grave. We snuck around back to spy on Frederick and Faith."

Zeke stopped again. Terror and revulsion turned his face into a mask of pain. He caught his breath. "Frederick wanted to eat her," he said loudly. "He wanted Faith to cook her own daughter," he said louder and shriller. His face was wild and he shook all over.

Everyone froze.

"Oh my," Simon said. Tears were streaming down all their faces at the horror of Zeke's story. Zeke laughed hysterically and jumped up in some sort of weird dance.

"We killed him," he screeched, "Lottie and Faith and I killed him."

The small group looked startled at the crazy little boy who was jumping up and down in glee; dancing his macabre jig. Suddenly he collapsed, his eyes rolling back in his head; his breathing was shallow.

"Let's go, boys," Hoss Woman said frantically. "Put him on a horse and let's go home."

They took turns helping Zeke who had never ridden a horse. He was a zombie, but followed their directions. They gave him water and hardtack which he sniffed suspiciously. Billy talked to him incessantly; told about the ranch; its occupants; and their plans for the future. When he ran out of breath, Hoss Woman took over, but Zeke kept turning to Billy. Simon and Joshua were very quiet. It was nightfall before they arrived. Minora ran out shouting.

"Billy, Billy, you have a son. He's small but he can yell."

Billy jumped down and ran to the bunkhouse.

Zeke became very agitated and tried to run away.

Joshua and Simon got him off the horse and took him by force to the bunkhouse kitchen where they fed him. Kate talked to him softly and gave him coffee which he liked. Zeke touched Kate's face gently, put his head on her chest and went to sleep.

Hoss Woman came in after helping Jimmy Jack unsaddle the horses and give them fresh water and feed. She told Zeke's story to Kate.

"What can we do with him?" Hoss Woman queried. "He is so damaged. What have I done?" She started to cry and Kate pulled her close so that both she and Zeke were cosseted in her arms. The Reverend and Shamus found them like that – all sleep.

The Reverend prayed softly and Shamus carried Zeke to the house with Hoss Woman with Kate stumbling behind. Zeke awoke and cried until Kate snuggled him and let him sleep with them all together. Hoss Woman

woke early and slipped quietly from the room. Picking up

clean clothes, she went to the pond to wash. Soon she was

joined by Billy, Simon, Joshua and Grace, They could

see Minora and Beatrice starting the morning repast.

Jimmy Jack came out of the barn, throwing them disgusted

looks. He wasn't much for bathing.

While they were eating breakfast, Shamus, Kate and

Zeke arrived. They had washed him and got him some

new clothes. Zeke ate. He kept a hand around his plate as

though he thought they might take it away. Hoss Woman

and Kate exchanged looks. Neither knew what to do with

him. Jimmy Jack came in and sat next to Zeke to eat.

Zeke eyed the grizzly old man warily.

"Wanna help me feed a foal?" Jimmy Jack asked

Zeke. "His mama don't want her and she needs to be

bottle fed, poor little girl."

"Ok," said Zeke and followed Jimmy Jack out.

Everyone started talking at once.

"Can he stay?"

"Should we tell Deputy Petey he's here?"

"How we gonna keep him a secret?"

"Can he read or write?"

"Did he shoot the Sheriff?"

On and on it went until Minora brought Billy's son out so that everyone could see him and take turns holding him. Zeke came in and looked at the baby. With a big grin, he turned to Billy and said, "He's good."

Everyone laughed but there were lots of chores to get caught up.

The Reverend had been working all week on his

sermon and when Sunday came, he preached of love and forgiveness and brotherhood. Simon sang and brought the congregation to tears; but it was Shamus and his hymn that had everyone humbled and breathless.

Sawhorses and boards were brought out for makeshift tables and Minora and Beatrice filled them quickly. They had been preparing food all day and night. Billy and Joshua had roasted a pig on an open spit and it smelled up the entire church yard. Mouths were watering. Everyone had brought food and he fiddler was tuning up.

Hoss Woman saw Deputy Petey talking to Zeke and she tried to reach them, but neighbors and town folk kept stopping her to tell her how much fun this was and how wonderful it was to have a church and a real preacher. She worried about what Zeke might say.

The Reverend held an evening service and then

everyone headed home. There were cheers and byes

called back and forth.

Henry lingered a while, but whatever was on his

mind stayed there and he left.

The next evening, Kate and Hoss Woman were on

the porch when Zeke came between them and held hands

with each of them.

"I've got a secret," he whispered.

Coffee Kate stood up quickly and gasped.

"My water broke, get Shamus."

Hoss Woman jumped up and ran fo Minora and

Beatrice. She yelled at Zeke to get Shamus from the

blacksmith shop. When Shamus arrived on the run, he

lifted her and carried her to the bunkhouse. When he came

out, he was white as a sheet. Zeke stood on the porch with

his fingers in his mouth. Hoss Woman went to tell Sarah

she would be cooking in the morning, found Jimmy Jack and told him the boys would have double chores. Grace offered to help Sarah in the morning if the Reverend Simon would watch the store and the smith. It was a long night.

When the first light showed over the hill, Hoss Woman and Zeke started the chores until Billy, Simon, Joshua and Jimmy Jack came out to help with the horses. The Reverend went to the store and smith. Shamus raced back and forth and refused to eat breakfast. He was so nervous. The women would not let him in no matter how loud Coffee Kate yelled.

Everyone started cheering when Minora and Beatrice came out to announce that Shamus and Kate had twin boys.

"Twins," beamed Shamus, "you mean two boys?"

He hurried in to see his sons and Kate.

With all the excitement, Hoss Woman had forgotten that Zeke had been ready to tell them a secret.

Chapter Nine (Jimmy Jack)

Hoss Woman woke one night covered with sweat and breathing heavy; what was wrong? She lay still thinking. Maybe it had been a nightmare. She went to the window but everything was quiet. Maybe she had heard the twins wanting a feeding. Hoss Woman wanted some coffee so she donned clothes and went to the kitchen, stoked the fire, and warmed some coffee. She took the tankard outside.

The horses in the corrals were restless and nervous. Something is wrong, thought Hoss Woman, something is definitely wrong.

Billy came from the bunkhouse. "What's up, sis?"

Hoss Woman shrugged and looke around. Billy took her cup and drank some coffee and handed it back.

"They sure are restless. I wonder why they spooked? Where's Jimmy Jack? He is usually up and checking on them."

Billy headed for the barn and when he didn't return, Hoss Woman went to look for him. Billy was kneeling beside the old man's body with tears rolling down his cheeks. Jimmy Jack had gone to his eternal reward. Hoss Woman gasped and knelt beside Billy, both crying for their loss.

They buried Jimmy Jack the next day. Reverend Singleton said a pray and Shamus sang a heart-rending hymn. The would all miss Jimmy Jack. They did their chores in subdued mood, ate quickly and dispersed quietly.

Chapter Ten (Who shot the Sheriff?)

One evening, Shamus and Hoss Woman were sitting on the porch. Coffee Kate was in the house feeding the twins. Bill, simon, Joshua, Mae, Zeke, Sara and Grace were swimming and splashing in the pond.

"Travelers," said Shamus.

Three women were limping and helping each other along. They were young and barely dressed in tattered clothe; their feet bleeding; their bodies were skinny and they looked half starved. Shamus and Hoss Woman hurried out to the road and helped them to the porch.

Minora and Beatrice came from the bunkhouse with plates of food and jugs of water. After the women ate, the one who appeared to be the leader thanked them and told the gang they had seen the ad. It had taken a long time to find their way.

All of the swimmers came out of the water; dressed and surrounded the women, Coffee Kate came out to see what the ruckus was about, plopping the twins in their father's lap.

"I'm Hannah, this is Maria and this is Prudence. We worked in a saloon for a man named Faro. He's a cruel man, so when we heard about work here, we ran away."

Maria said, "You won't make us go back, will you?" She had a Mexican accent.

"Of course not," said Hoss Woman.

"Why don't we get you cleaned up and some new clothes," Minora said.

Simon took Maria's hand and asked, "Can you swim?"

Maria shook her head.

Joshua took Prudence; Grace took Hannah and they all went to the pond where they washed the women's bloody feet and some of the trail dust off. Billy and Mae came with pants, flannel shirts and suspenders. The girls looked aghast, but with help they put on the clothes. Maria and Prudence giggled at each other's strange attire and Hannah smiled.

Shamus was singing lullabies to the boys and Mae brought out her son to enjoy the music.

After coffee, which the ladies enjoyed, Minora showed the girls where they could sleep. She and Beatrice went to their rooms; tired from a long day. It would be a blessing to have more help.

Billy told Hoss Woman and Kate, "I think we should make a horse run – right?"

Both women nodded. The expenses were mounting fast with the expansion and their school and library were not completed. They would need money to pay the men and provide supplies.

Billy said, "I'll organize it. I don't think we need to hire any men from town. Can you gals handle all the chores?"

Coffee Kate chortled, "Been doing that long before you."

Billy grinned.

Minora and Beatrice reported that the three new women were good at sewing, cooking and cleaning, but no farm skills such as riding, tending garden or feeding horses.

"You can teach them," said Hoss Woman.

Joshua started riding lessons in the afternoon and all

three girls seemed to enjoy it. Only Hannah could read and write a little.

Coffee Kate and Hoss Woman were alone, sipping coffee, on the porch. Everyone else had retired.

"Have you heard from Captain?" Kate asked.

"No," said Hoss Woman sadly.

The very next day, Captain arrived with two soldiers. Hoss Woman ran to him and he dismounted quickly, hugging her closely. The two soldiers remained mounted. The Captain drew Hoss Woman into the barn and kissed her.

"I can't stay long," he said. "We have orders to go to Colorado Territory and will be gone a while, but I had to see you."

Hoss Woman sadly waved goodbye as they rode away.

The hot days of summer dragged along. Billy and Josh taught Prudence, Maria, Zeke and Hannah how to herd the horses; rope the horses and make rope halters. Early in late summer, the six wranglers left to collect new mustangs. Hoss Woman worked harder than ever. The store was busy every day and Hoss Woman helped Grace fill orders and keep supplies in stock. Their biggest argument had been about alcohol. Hoss Women refused to stock it. Shamus disagreed. The Reverend sided with Hoss Woman; Minora and Beatrice sided with Shamus. Kate said nothing. Mae and Grace weren't sure. The matter was on hold until the herders returned.

Every Sunday the people from town came to the church services led by Josiah. Simon or Shamus sang. Occasionally there was a wedding or a funeral. Kate and Shamus had the twins baptized but Mae wanted to wait until Billy returned.

Billy, Zeke and the girls were long over due and everyone worried about them. Thy missed Jimmy Jack and Hoss Woman visited his grave with wild flowers, wondering if he had a family somewhere. He had never said.

In the evening the tired group would gather on the porch to drink Kate's marvelous coffee, gossip and play with the three babies. Sometimes Henry rode over and usually Shamus sang. Hoss Woman was very quiet and Kate was worried about her.

Early one morning a trooper rode up and handed letters to Hoss Woman, He declined to dismount or eat, and giving Hoss Woman a sly glance, rode off in the direction of the fort. She put the letters under the cushion of the rocker and went about the chores.

At noon they all gathered at the corrals to witness

Joshua, Bill, Zeke, Prudence, Maria and Hannah, along with three tall strangers, bring in a large herd of mustangs. The corrals filled up quick and were jammed packed. Hoss Woman made a mental note that they would need to fence off a large area of pasture for the future. One of the wranglers roped the stud with expertise and panache and led him to a small shelter outside the last corral. The stud was kicking and fighting and calling to his ladies. He was a magnificent black with a white blaze on his forehead.

Minora and Beatrice retreated to the bunkhouse kitchen to start a meal; Grace closed the store and Shamus left the blacksmith shop.

At Billy's insistence, his crew threw off their clothes and jumped into the pond. The new wranglers shyly went in clothes and all. They ate heartily and praised the cooking, joking and laughing. Maria seemed especially friendly with one certain cowboy and Billy winked at Hoss Woman when she raised her eyebrow. The rest of the day was spent talking about the mustangs and plans to expand the horse area.

It was a lively bunch that gathered for coffee that evening The tall, rangy cowboy that led the wranglers was named Jake and he had joined with Billy's group because there were too many to handle.

"Jake is working for five mustangs and the stud," Billy informed them. "We don't need another one. The men are working for five mustangs each." Billy was proud he had worked this out.

"Good," praised Kate.

Shamus and Simon sang and one of the wranglers named Slim, played the mouth organ. Maria and her beau disappeared. The babies slept. Hoss Woman took out the letters, the trooper had delivered. Three were addressed to the Captain and the fourth was a white envelope with a black border. It was addressed to Mrs. Captain. Hoss Woman stared at it as she opened it with trembling fingers; dropped it to the ground; and disappeared into the house.

Billy picked it up and read: "The United States Army regrets to inform you of the death of Captain John Thomas in a skirmish at Settler's Mound where he is buried. His personal belongings will be delivered to you."

Hoss Woman stayed in her room the next day, but the day after she appeared and did her share of the work as usual.

Billy asked to speak to Kate and Hoss Woman alone and they gathered in the far corner of the bunkhouse kitchen.

"Jake has asked me if he could rent or buy the pasture on the other side of the brook. He would start his own horse ranch there with his stud and five mares. I told him I would let him know. The wrangler called Knobby wants to marry Maria and work with Jake. The third wrangler, Slim, is leaving tomorrow."

Kate and Hoss Woman sat silent thinking and mulling it over in their minds.

Hoss Woman said, "I don't want to sell any of our land; we have worked too hard to get this far."

Kate said, "He appears to be a fine fellow. I don't think he knows there is another pasture beyond the stand of trees nearer to Henry's ranch. That would be more suitable. Let's rent it to him for a small fee."

Billy nodded. He and Jake rode out and checked on the suitability and agreed on the payments. Jake seemed pleased with the arrangement. Billy took him to meet

Henry and let Henry know he would have another

neighbor. Billy showed him the store and said he could

order supplies from there or in town and Jake admired the

blacksmith shop.

Hoss Woman was not at the evening gathering and

Jake wandered away looking for her. She was sitting on a

stone, looking out over the ranch and watching the sun dip

behind the mountains.

Jake sat down next to her. "I'm sorry you lost your

husband," he said.

Hoss Woman said, "He was not my husband; that's

just an Army mix-up, but I really liked him." She smiled

at Jake. "Want to go swimming?" she asked.

Jake blushed red but went along with Hoss Woman

to the pond. It was all ready in use by the young folks.

Jake was surprised that no one was modest and just played and splashed, mostly naked. Hoss Woman took off her clothes and grabbed his hand.

"You aren't bashful are you?"

"Of course I'm not," Jake said, knowing it was a lie.

They enjoyed the cool water and Jake could swim a little. He splashed Hoss Woman and jumped away when she tried to splash him back. It was a fun evening.

A few days later, Betty Sue and Mary arrived in a buggy. Hoss Woman and Jake had just sat down to have coffee and enjoy a slight breeze before evening chores and dinner.

Betty Sue accepted coffee. Mary hugged Hoss Woman and waved to Zeke and Billy working with the horses. They quickly came over and hugged her too.

My, she is pretty, Hoss Woman thought. She looks

just like our Ma.

"We came to say good-bye," Betty Sue said primly. "The Sheriff passed last night. I will miss him, but I won't miss this town. Mary needs to go to finishing school and I want to go East."

Billy said, "Mary should stay here with her family."

"But I haven't been part of this family for years, and I want to go."

"So you shall," said Hoss Woman sadly. "Please send me your address so we can write. If you need money, please let me know."

Betty Sue looked chaste and Coffee Kate realized she had come to request funds. She went inside to the hidey-hole in the fireplace.

Quiet Zeke spoke, "The Sheriff died?"

"Yes," sniffled Betty Sue, holding a scented

handkerchief to her nose.

"I know who shot him," said Zeke.

Everyone stopped short. Coffee Kate's mouth dropped open.

"How do you know?" Bill demanded angrily, afraid for Zeke.

"I was there."

Betty Sue let out a screech. "I always knew you had something to do with it. I'll see you hang," She grabbed him by the neck, shaking him.

"Wait a dang minute" Billy said, "Let's hear what he has to say."

Betty Sue gave Zeke a push and he stumbled and fell backwards. There was a huge crack as Zeke's head connected with the porch post and he slumped over with blood gushing from the back of his head.

Billy was the first to reach him and he pulled off his shirt and wadded it over Zeke's wound, cradling his brother.

Zeke opened his eyes. "It was Mr. Feathers," he said weakly, "The Sheriff and he were arguing because he wanted the Sheriff to put Hoss Woman out of business and the Sheriff refused, so he shot him."

Billy and Jake put Zeke in the buckboard and headed for town.

Betty Sue was crying. "I didn't mean to hurt him." Mary put her arms around her and led her to the carriage. Kate followed and gave Mary a pouch filled with coins. No one said goodbye.

After Billy and Jake left Zeke with the doctor, they went to Deputy Petey and told him the story.

"Are you pressing charges against Betty Sue?" he

asked, shaking his head.

"No," said Billy, "Let her go."

Deputy Petey, Jake and Billy went to the doctor's office. Zeke was sleeping and the doctor told them he should spend the night., They could wait until the next day to get a statement and take him home. Billy and Jake found everyone on the porch waiting to hear the news.

Jake took Hoss Woman's hand and they went for a walk in the moonlight. He kissed her gently and she laid her head on his shoulder. The stars were out in full force.

The next day Zeke reported his story to Deputy Petey.

"Why didn't you tell someone before now?" asked Petey.

Zeke cried, "when I came to town, Mr. Feathers cocked his finger at me like it was a gun. He moved it to

Billy. He might kill my whole family." Poor Zeke, thought Billy. He has been carrying a heavy burden.

"Is the grocer in jail?" he asked.

"Not yet," said the deputy. "You'll have to testify and say everything before the judge. Can you do that?"

"We'll be there with you," said Billy giving his little brother a friendly pat.

The store was locked up tighter than a drum.

"Looks like he skedaddled," said Deputy Petey. "I'll put a wanted poster out on him."

"Make the reward one thousand dollars," said Billy. "I'll cover it."

"I hear Mary is going East," gossiped Petey.

Billy said "She wants to go to finishing school. Why would anyone want to leave here?" He gestured at the mountains rising outside of town.

Deputy Petey shook hands with Billy and Zeke. The went to the stables and retrieved their horse and buggy and drove home. Everyone fussed over Zeke, who proudly displayed his wound.

Chapter Eleven (Life Continues On)

Summer dragged on, then winter and finally spring blossomed on the desert. Beatrice and Reverend Singleton were having an argument. Grace and Simon had come to them and asked to be married. Beatrice was against it.

"I'm not against people of color," she exclaimed vehemently. "I just think Grace could do better."

"And where will she get this better person?" asked the Reverend., "They are in love and they will run away if we don't sanction this union and we won't know if they are doing well or not."

No one else offered an opinion or took sides except Mae who sided with Grace and was angry with Beatrice. The disagreement caused bad feelings all around

Jake and Hoss Woman were together so often, that Kate began to speculate about a wedding. She wanted Hoss Woman to be as happy as she and Shamus were.

Billy's herds had increased and buyers came often, some from long distances. They knew they would get good stock at a fair price. Jake's smaller herd was growing and he trained them well. Billy's son, Micah, was walking and talking and the twins and he were fast friends. Micah loved his 'Unca-eke' as he called Zeke and the three boys followed him everywhere.

Chapter Twelve (Grandfather)

A very strange sight appeared on the road from town. A large fancy red and black barouche drawn by two lovely black horses and driven by a small man dressed in a green and gold suit and a green hat, pulled into the yard and stopped in front of the porch.

The tiny man called down, "What is the name of this place?"

Hoss Woman and Jake were sitting on the porch. She stood and answered, "This is the Harmon Horse Ranch."

She waited patiently as he opened a small window and relayed the information to his passenger. He hopped down and opened the carriage door, putting steps down and taking the hand of a tall, lean older gentleman dressed in a gray suit complete with watch fob and gray tie.

The little green man turned and bowed to Hoss

Woman. He announced that his passenger was Talbot Freeman from Boston.

Hoss Woman was the first to react to this strange apparition. "Grandfather," she cried out and ran to him to hug him. His face was stony and he did not return the hug.

"I am seeking my daughter Lucinda Freeman."

Hoss Woman corrected him. "Lucinda Harmon, and she has been dead for a long, long time. She died when Mary was born."

"Mary," said Talbot stiffly.

"My little sister, but, oh my, I am forgetting my manners. Come and sit down. My partner makes the world's best coffee." She sent Jake to collect Zeke and Billy.

She grabbed her grandfather's hand and pulled him to the porch. Everyone gathered around and Hoss Woman said, "This is Billy and Zeke your grandsons and this is

Micah your great grandson. Micah climbed into his lap,

sucking his two fingers. Talbot looked aghast at the crowd

and at the little boy on his lap.

Billy called to the little man in the green suit, "Take

your horses to the barn and feed and water them." The

man looked shocked and glanced at Talbot, who motioned

him to go.

Mae joined them and Billy said, "This is my wife

Mae."

How many of you are there?" asked Talbot

distastefully. "Where is that fool that stole my daughter

away? How did she die? Don't you read? I have been

advertising for years."

Everyone was quiet and then Hoss Woman replied,

"you have four grandchildren; I am Hester, this is Billy

and Zeke. Mary is at finishing school in the East. The 'fool' ran off with a dance hall dolly, after Ma died giving birth to Mary, leaving us alone to starve. We survived with hard work and planning."

The Reverend and Simon showed up and Kate handed them coffee. The tiny man and Talbot refused the drinks.

"This is my pastor and his son."

"Welcome," said the Reverend holding out his hand. Talbot ignored it.

"Fetch the carriage," Talbot ordered the little green man. "I want to go lie down." His skin looked pasty and pale, he pushed Micah off his lap unceremoniously.

His little green man brought the huge carriage around.

"Wait," said Hoss Woman, clearly distraught.

"Where are you going? You have to stay here."

"To the hotel," he directed the green man who was helping him up the steps.

"Well, I never," said Coffee Kate upset.

"Come boys," ordered Hoss Woman, "We are going after him and I will give him a piece of my mind. How dare he treat us like that? No wonder Ma ran away from that horrid man."

The saddled three horses and the Harmons went to town, riding straight to the hotel.

"What room is Talbot in?" demanded Billy of the hotel clerk.

"Rooms," he said, holding up three fingers, "six, seven and eight. He said he didn't want to be disturbed and I wouldn't if I were you."

"Well, you're not!" snapped Hoss Woman and the

trio climbed the stairs and banged loudly on six, seven and eight.

Talbot opened the door saying, "I thought I told you...." but stopped when the three Harmons pushed him aside and strode into his room.

"How dare you treat us like that!" yelled Hoss Woman. "We are highly respected in this community. We took a ragtag shack and turned it into one of the finest horse ranches in the West. We can buy and sell you like that!" and she snapped her fingers under his nose. "Ma died and left us destitute. No one would treat us the way you do, you old goat. I can see why Ma ran away, you fool, and we are leaving too. Don't ever come near us again without apologizing."

"What do you expect," said Talbot, "dressed like that." He turned red with anger, "and ragamuffins hanging around."

"How dare you!" Billy said. "You are despicable!"

They turned and stormed out. The little green man was standing in the hallway, his eyes as big as saucers.

He said, "Miss Hester, he usually isn't so bad. It has been a long trip from Boston."

"You know where we live if he wants to apologize," she said stiffly.

The little green man shook his head.

Hoss Woman beat both Zeke and Billy back to the ranch. No one asked what had happened in town and chores were done quickly and quietly.

No one came to the porch for coffee, so Coffee Kate, Shamus, Jake and Hoss Woman sat quietly rocking and sipping, lost deep in thought.

Zeke approached them. "Grace has the store, Billy and Joshua take care of horses; Reverend and Simon have the church; Minora and Beatrice sew and cook for everyone; Shamus has the smith, you and Coffee oversee everyone, but what do I have?"

"What do you want?" asked Shamus.

"The library," he said, "I want to read books. You built it and you left it empty."

"He's right," said Kate.

Early next morning Hoss Woman sought out Jake and told him what she had stayed awake most of the night, planning. Hoss Woman liked Jake's common sense and often used his thoughtful, quiet demeanor as a sounding board. He offered no changes to her plan and sought out Billy and Joshua to go to town. He wanted to check with the newspaper man how to order books.

"It looks like someone has to go to St. Louis," Jake said that evening. "We need to order books and other supplies."

"Hey, sis," said Billy, "Why don't you go – you and Coffee and Shamus and Jake. We can handle the ranch and the kids."

Hoss Woman looked at Kate.

"Let's do it," said Shamus. "We haven't been off this ranch in years."

Hoss Woman looked at Jake who winked at her.

"Best idea," he said.

Everyone was sleeping when Jake tapped on her bedroom window. "Let's go swimming," he said when she pulled back the curtain.

They went to the pond, giggling and undressing at the same time, falling over their clothes and into the water.

They splashed each other and thoroughly enjoyed the cool water. They heard splashing and turned to see Shamus and Kate wrapped in each other's arms. A full moon illuminated the pond.

It wasn't long before the preparations had been made and the four of them hitched the wagon. Minora and Beatrice packed food, clothes and blankets for them. Jake tied his horse to the rear of the wagon and then Hoss Woman asked him to bring along her pinto. The trip was fun and they camped out under the stars.

Hoss Woman had never been to the city before, but Shamus had, so he directed them where to stable their horses and found a good hotel where they unpacked. They wandered around the bustling city. Hoss Woman's eyes were huge and Jake delighted in teasing his country bumpkin about the sights, the smells and the strange scenery.

While Coffee Kate and Hoss Woman shopped and ordered supplies, Shamus and Jake got drunk at the hotel bar. By the time they met up, everyone was hungry so they went and ate at the fanciest restaurant in town.

The wagon was packed with gifts and presents and the supplies had been ordered and shipment arranged. Coffee Kate and Hoss Woman had ordered books for the library which would be shipped from Chicago and New York. They would arrive several weeks from now.

The four friends reluctantly left St. Louis and traveled home slowly. Jake and Hoss Woman rode away from the wagon in early evening seeking privacy as well as affording Coffee Kate and Shamus the same. Jake spread a blanket on the ground and built a small fire to warm coffee. He pulled a ring from his pocket and asked

Hoss Woman to marry him.

"I will treasure you all my life," he vowed and kissed her fervently.

"Oh, yes," said Hoss Woman happily.

Shamus and his wife were happy to hear the news and they continued their journey teasing and singing.

On Sunday, the Reverend Singleton solemnly announced there would be a wedding the following week and another the week after (Beatrice had finally relented and agreed to Grace and Simon marrying). Congratulations were given as people laid out their Sunday picnics. Shamus, then Simon, sang beautiful hymns. All week was busy with chores, busting broncs and wedding preparations. Jake and Hoss Woman were lost in each other's eyes and took a lot of teasing.

The wedding was lovely and the happy couple

received numerous compliments and well wishes. The honeymoon couple went to town and rented a hotel room for their wedding night. Needless to say, Talbot was long gone, and never responded to the wedding announcement.

The next evening, Beatrice and Minora prepared another feast for everyone. Jake come in from feeding horses and looked around for Hoss Woman. A momentary frown crossed his handsome features, and he took a seat. Everyone came in and Henry came from his ranch. The Reverend said the blessing.

"Where's Hoss Woman," asked Jake?

"Where's Zeke?" Billy said, "It's not like him to miss a meal."

"I saw her going to the library when I rode up," said Henry.

"Why would she go there?" Jake queried.

He left and as he approached the empty building, he spied a strange horse tied in the woods. He had a very odd feeling and returned to the bunkhouse kitchen where he motioned for Billy, Joshua and Shamus to come out. He told them what he had seen and they surrounded the building. Zeke cried out and they moved to a window and peeked over the sill.

Jake's heart skipped a beat. Hoss Woman was tied to a chair and Mr. Feathers was holding a knife to Zeke's throat, Shamus went to the front and kicked in the door with Billy and at the same time Jake and Joshua crashed through the back door.

Feathers yelled, "Stop or I'll kill him." Jake kicked out and the knife went flying. Shamus and Billy grabbed Feathers and Jake untied Hoss Woman.,

They hogtied Feathers so he lay on his belly with his

arms and legs tied behind his back. He looked very uncomfortable. Joshua and Billy raced into town to bring Deputy Petey back to pick him up.

As the family gathered on the porch for Kate's world-famous coffee, they all gave special thanks. Jake rubbed Hoss Woman's wrists that were bruised from the tight ropes that Feathers had used. Everyone retold the story of the rescue and all were happy they were safe.

Hoss Woman gazed around the ranch with grateful eyes; her husband; her brothers; her friends and workers; and thought of Talbot in his lonely Boston mansion. He has no idea what he is missing, she thought.

THE END